THE
CHRISTMAS PAGEANT

illustrated by Tomie de Paola

text from the stories of
Matthew and Luke

Winston Press

ISBN: 0-03-046356-4
Library of Congress Catalog Card Number: 78-69869

Winston Press
430 Oak Grove
Minneapolis, MN 55403

7902542C

Long ago, on the very first Christmas night, something wonderful happened. A special baby was born. Many, many people had waited a long time for this baby. Tonight in our play we will celebrate the story of his birth.

Here is how the story began. A woman named Mary and her husband Joseph lived in the town of Nazareth in a place called Galilee. Mary was going to have a baby. She and Joseph knew that this baby would be special. Happily they made many plans for the baby's birth.

Then news came that changed their plans. Their king wanted to know how many people lived in his kingdom. So he asked all the people to go to their hometowns to be counted. Mary and Joseph had to travel from Nazareth to Bethlehem.

The trip was long and hard. It was especially hard for Mary, since it was almost time for her baby to be born. But at last Mary and Joseph arrived in Bethlehem. How crowded it was! Many others had come to be counted, too.

Mary and Joseph were very tired from their trip. So they looked for a place to rest for the night. But all the rooms in Bethlehem were full. "What will we do now?" they wondered.

Then Joseph found a small barn. "Mary can rest here," he thought. Joseph swept out the barn and prepared a place for Mary to sleep. Then he put fresh, sweet-smelling straw in the manger where the donkeys and oxen ate. "Let's use this manger for our baby's bed," he suggested to Mary.

The barn was quiet and peaceful. All the animals went to sleep. "Thank you, Joseph, for finding this place," said Mary.

That night the baby was born. At first he cried and woke up the animals. But then Mary sang to him and wrapped him in a warm cloth. She laid him on the soft straw in the manger, and the baby went to sleep. "God wants us to call our baby Jesus," Mary said to Joseph. Mary and Joseph were very happy, for they knew that God sent this child to do wonderful things for people.

That same night, some shepherds heard about the special baby. They were taking care of their sheep on the hillsides near Bethlehem. Some of them were huddled around the campfire to keep warm. Some were talking. Some were sleeping.

Just then, an angel appeared to the shepherds. They were so surprised and frightened that they cried out. The sleeping shepherds woke up. "Don't be afraid," said the angel. "I have good news for you. News that will make you very happy. A special baby has been born. He will show you how much God loves you. Go to Bethlehem. You will find the baby there. He is wrapped in a warm cloth and is lying in a manger."

Suddenly, many more angels appeared to the shepherds. "God is wonderful," sang the angels, "and all people will be filled with peace."

Well! The shepherds were so excited they hardly knew what to say to one another. Should they leave their sheep and go to Bethlehem? Could they find that baby among so many people? "Come," said one of the shepherds. "Let's hurry and find the child. He must be very special if angels came to tell us about him."

In Bethlehem the shepherds looked up one street and down the other. At last they found Mary and Joseph and the baby. Jesus was sleeping peacefully on his bed of straw just as the angel had said. When the shepherds saw Jesus they were filled with joy.

Far away, three wise men were looking for the baby, too. They had seen a bright, new star in the East. When they saw the star, they knew that someone special had been born. So the wise men left their faraway lands to search for the baby. They traveled day and night. Each night they looked into the sky to see if the star was still there. Some nights they could not see it. Then they asked, "Where can we find the special child who has just been born?" But no one could tell them.

Then one night the star shone brighter than ever before. "Hurrah!" shouted the wise men. "We must be very near." They followed the star to the place where Mary and Joseph and Jesus were.

As they looked at Jesus, a feeling came over the wise men that made them kneel down before him. Then each wise man offered Jesus a birthday gift.

"I bring you gold," said one.

"I bring you frankincense," said another.

"I bring you myrrh," said the third.

Jesus smiled at them. The wise men could hardly wait to tell everyone about this special child.

These things happened a long time ago. But every year we celebrate the birthday of Jesus, who has shown us how much God loves us and how we should love one another. We are glad you celebrated with us.